To my good friend Irene, who advised me to "just do it!" —R. T.
To Karma Lilian Kendall, who is niece number one. —G. L.

Text © 2004 by Roseanne Thong.
Illustrations © 2004 by Grace Lin.

Book design by Sara Gillingham.
Typeset in Melior.
The illustrations in this book were rendered in gouache.
Manufactured in China.

Library of Congress Cataloging-in-Publication Data
Thong, Roseanne.
One is a drummer / by Roseanne Thong ; illustrated by Grace Lin.
p. cm.
Summary: A young girl numbers her discoveries in the world around her,
from one dragon boat to four mahjong players to ten bamboo stalks.
ISBN 0-8118-3772-6
[1. Counting. 2. Chinese Americans—Fiction. 3. Stories in rhyme.] I.Lin, Grace, ill. II. Title.
PZ8.3.T328On 2004
[E]—dc22
2003010810

Distributed in Canada by Raincoast Books
9050 Shaughnessy Street, Vancouver, British Columbia V6P 6E5

10 9 8 7 6 5 4 3 2 1

Chronicle Books LLC
85 Second Street, San Francisco, California 94105

www.chroniclekids.com

One Is a Drummer

A BOOK OF NUMBERS

written by Roseanne Thong ✿ illustrated by Grace Lin

chronicle books · san francisco

One is a drummer
 One is a race
One is a dragon boat
 that wins first place!

One is a tail
and a cool, wet nose
One is a tongue
that tickles my toes

Two are the greetings
on our wall
"Luck" and "Fortune"
for us all

大吉

Three are the steamers
Three are the buns
Three are the egg tarts—
here they come!

Four are the friends
who play mahjong
Four are the songbirds
that chirp along

Four are the seasons
I know them all
Spring, summer,
winter and fall

Five are the fish balls
on a stick
Five are the fingers
that I lick

Six are the horses
on a merry-go-round
Six are the children
going up and down!

Seven is the number
of days in a week
What day is today?
Let's take a peek!

六月 June

星期日
day

星期一
Monday

星期二
Tuesday

星期三
Wednesday

星期四
Thursday

星期五
Friday

星期
S

1

2

3

4

8

9

10

17

15

16

23

22

龍舟節
DRAGON BOAT
FESTIVAL

28

29

Eight are the napkins
Eight are the dishes
Eight are the candles
for making wishes

**Eight are the Chinese
Immortals of old
Eight are the precious
gifts they hold**

Nine colored swimsuits
Nine pairs of feet
Nine are the children
escaping the heat

Ten are the stalks
 of green bamboo
Ten cool stepping stones
 to walk on through

There are so many numbers
at home and at play
How many have
you counted today?

Dragon Boat Festival: During this celebration, people remember the famous poet Qu Yuan who died long ago. He is said to have leaped into a river when an evil king captured his kingdom. Fishermen tried to save Qu Yuan by beating on drums and splashing their oars to keep the water dragons away. When they realized it was too late, they scattered rice dumplings into the river so that his soul would never be hungry. A special kind of rice dumpling called *zhong-zi* is eaten to remember Qu Yuan. It is made of glutinous rice and wrapped in bamboo leaves.

❁

Dragon Boats: Complete with ferocious heads, scales and long, thin bodies, these boats are raced during the Dragon Boat Festival. A drummer sits up front and beats out the pace, as rowers follow with their oars.

❁

New Year Greetings: At the New Year, bright red banners carrying wishes for luck, good fortune and new beginnings are hung on the walls and doors of homes, restaurants and public places.

❁

Dim Sum: A Cantonese term meaning "a little heart," dim sum refers to little snacks or treats that are eaten with Chinese tea for breakfast or lunch. They are often served three at a time in bamboo steamers. Some popular dim sum items include shrimp dumplings, barbecued pork buns, meatballs and egg tarts.

❁

Mahjong: This traditional Chinese game requires four players and uses 144 rectangular tiles made of plastic or wood. The tiles come in suits of bamboo, dots, numbers, winds, flowers, dragons and directions (north, south, east, west), and make a delightful clicking noise when they are laid on the table.

❁

Eight Immortals: These legendary beings are based on real people who lived long ago. The immortals carry Taoist symbols: a basket of flowers, a sword, castanets, a fan, a gourd, a flute, a tube drum and a lotus blossom.

❁

Bamboo: This plant is favored by Chinese in home and temple gardens. There is a saying that people should try to grow up straight and strong, just like bamboo.